Bob's Big Book of Stories

Bob's Boots

One morning Bob walked into his front room carrying a big box.

"Look, Finn!" he said excitedly. "The postman has just delivered this. I wonder what's inside?" Finn pressed his nose up against his glass tank and watched Bob open the box.

"My new boots have arrived!" cried Bob, holding them up for Finn to see. "What do you think of them?" he asked.

The goldfish did a back-flip. **Splash!** He really liked Bob's new boots!

"I think I'll wear my new boots to work," said Bob.

When he walked out into the yard, Wendy was giving the machines their jobs for the day.

"Lofty, you're with Bob today," she said. "Muck and Scoop, you're with me."

"Morning, Wendy," called Bob.

"Morning, Bob," Wendy replied.

Bob walked around the yard proudly.

"What do you think of my new boots?" he asked them.

"They're very smart," replied Wendy.

Bob stopped and looked around.

"Can anyone hear squeaking?" he asked.

"I can't hear anything," said Lofty.

Bob started to walk again and the squeaking came back.

Squeak, squeak, squeak!

"I can hear it now," said Wendy.

"Hee, hee!" giggled Dizzy.
"It sounds like mice."

Lofty started to shake all over.
"Ooohhh! Don't say that, Dizzy.
I'm scared of mice!"

As Bob walked towards Wendy, the squeaking got louder and louder.

"Ah ha! I think I know where it's coming from," said Wendy.

"Where?" asked Bob.

"Your boots!" laughed Wendy. "They need wearing in, to soften up the leather."

"You sound like you need oiling, Bob!" chuckled Scoop.

"I think I'll walk to the job today," said Bob. "I need to wear my new boots in!"

"Come on, Lofty!" he said, and waved goodbye to the others as they set off in the opposite direction.

Lofty clattered slowly along with Bob walking behind him, carrying his lunch box.

Squeak, squeak, squeak!

Further up the lane, Bird was listening to Travis and Spud, who were trying to work out the quickest way to Bob's yard.

"You go left at the crossroads," said Spud.

"I'm sure it's right..." muttered Travis.

"No, no, no!" cried Spud.

Just then, Farmer Pickles came past, so they asked him to settle the argument.

"They say the quickest way is usually as the crow flies," he replied. "It means the quickest way to get anywhere is to go in a straight line."

"Come on, Travis," said Farmer Pickles, "We've got work to do."

When they had gone, Spud turned to Bird and boasted, "I can run faster than any old bird can fly! I'll race you to Bob's yard!"

"Toot, toot!" cried Bird as he flew off.

In a nearby field, Lofty was trying to lift a heavy gate, but the strong wind was making it a bit tricky.

"Careful now," said Bob as he helped lower it into place.

"Phew! Time for lunch!" said Bob as he opened his lunch box.

"Oooh, what have you got today, Bob?" Lofty asked.

"My favourites! Cheese and chutney sandwiches and a big cream bun," Bob replied.

Suddenly a gust of wind blew the paper napkin from the top of Bob's sandwiches.

"Whooah!" cried Bob as he chased after it.

Meanwhile, Spud and Bird were racing across the countryside. Spud stopped when he noticed Bob's lunch box with the sandwiches and big cream bun inside.

"Mmmmm!" he said as he nibbled the sandwich. He was just about to take a big bite out of the cream bun when he spotted Bird flying away.

"I'd better save this bun until I get to Bob's yard," he said, racing off after Bird.

In the next field, Bob was still chasing after the paper napkin.

Squeak, squeak, squeak!

Three little mice heard the noise and thought it might be a friend! They jumped up and followed the sound of Bob's boots.

Finally, Bob managed to catch the napkin and went back to his lunch box, followed by the mice. When he got back he couldn't believe his eyes.

"Hey! Who's been eating my sandwiches?" he cried. "And my cream bun's gone! Have you seen it, Lofty?"

Lofty was just about to say he hadn't seen the sandwiches, when he spotted the three little mice peeping out from behind Bob's new boots.

"Aaaargghh!" he shrieked as he darted down the road.

"M... m... m... mice!"

"Mice?" said Bob. "Where?" But the little mice had scurried around behind Bob's back.

Bob chased after Lofty and the mice chased after Bob's squeaky boots!

"Come back, Lofty!" cried Bob.

Squeak, squeak, squeak!

Wendy, Muck and Scoop were filling a skip with rubbish from an old kitchen, when Bird zipped overhead, followed by Spud.

"Hello, Wendy!" called Spud. "Can't stop! Bye!"

"What is going on?" puzzled Wendy.

Back at the yard Roley was snoozing and Dizzy was playing, when suddenly Lofty came roaring in.

"Umm, what's the matter, Lofty?" rumbled Roley sleepily.

"M... m... mice!" stammered Lofty.

"They're chasing me!"

Bob rushed into the yard after Lofty.

"Lofty, there aren't any mice. Look!" said Bob, turning around. But this time the mice stayed still and he spotted them.

"Oooh," said Bob. "Lofty, you were right!"

The three little brown mice looked up at Bob.

Bob walked round in a circle and the mice followed him.

"Ha, ha! Look! They like my squeaky boots, don't they?"

"I don't like mice though," quivered Lofty.

Just then, Bird came whizzing into the yard and landed on Lofty.

Spud dashed in a moment later, gasping for breath.

"I've beaten Bird!" he cried.

"Toot, toot!" whistled Bird proudly.

"Oh, no," grumbled Spud as he spotted Bird. "But at least I can eat my cream bun."

"That's my bun, isn't it?" Bob asked sternly. "You know you shouldn't take other people's things without asking."

"Sorry, Bob," mumbled Spud. Feeling embarrassed, he stared at the ground where he saw the three hungry mice looking up at him.

"Go away!" he shouted.

As Wendy, Muck and Scoop turned into the yard, they saw Spud running down the road with the three mice scampering after him.

"Leave me alone!" Spud yelled.

"**Squeak, squeak, squeak!**" went the mice as they followed him down the road.

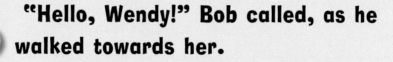

"Hello, Wendy!" Bob called, as he walked towards her.

"Bob! Your boots have stopped squeaking," said Wendy.

"I must have worn them in with all the running about I've been doing," Bob chuckled.

"Have you had a busy day?" Wendy asked.
"Not really," Bob replied. "You could say it's been as quiet as a mouse!"

THE END!

Spud the Dragon

"**R**ight, team, today we're working at Mrs Potts's house," said Bob, as he popped a roll of material into Muck's digger.

"Bob, what's that pink stuff?" Muck asked.

"It's insulating material for Mrs Potts's loft," explained Wendy. "It will stop the heat from escaping through the roof."

"Can we fix it?" asked Scoop.

"Yes, we can!" replied Muck, Dizzy, Wendy and Bob.

"Er, yeah... I think so," said Lofty.

Over at the school, Spud was delivering a ladder to Mrs Percival.

"Ah, thank you, Spud," she said. "This will come in handy for the school play," and she dashed off to get everything ready.

On his way out of the school-yard, Spud noticed a pile of dressing up clothes on a table.

"Ha ha! Look at all these goodies," he said, as he grabbed an eyepatch and headscarf.

"Ahoy! Beware of Spud the Pirate! A-har!" he cried, grabbing a cutlass and swishing it around.

Then Spud spotted a hobby horse and cowboy hat on the table, and instantly changed into 'Spud the Lone Ranger'.

"Away...!" he shouted, as he galloped through the yard, bumping into a big, green costume.

"Cor! What's this?" he said, as he crawled inside, and became...

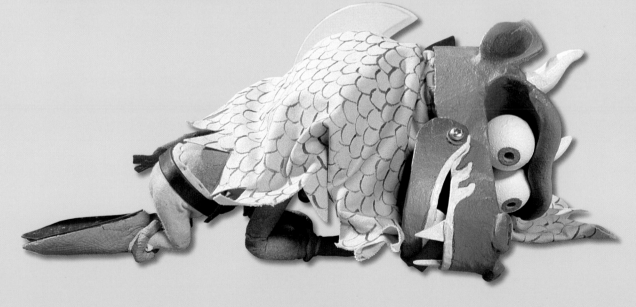

...Spud the Dragon!

"Roarrrrr!" cried Spud, as he raced away. "I'm sure Mrs Percival won't mind if I borrow this costume for a bit." Spud the Dragon saw Muck on his way back to the yard.

"Hee hee! Time for some fun!" chuckled Spud.

"Wh-h-h-o are you?" stammered Muck.

"I'm a magic dragon," Spud answered. "I'll grant you a wish if you close your eyes."

So Muck closed his eyes and thought hard.

"I wish," said Muck, excitedly, "I wish I was twice as big as I am now, so that I could shift lots and lots of mud."

Spud was trying hard not to giggle as he drew a big black nose on Muck's face, without him knowing.

"Mmm," continued Muck, "or how about... I wish I wasn't ever scared of the dark..."

Spud added long, stripey cat's whiskers to Muck's face.

"Keep your eyes closed!" whispered Spud. And then he ran off!

"Hello?" said Muck. "Mr Dragon?" Muck opened his eyes slowly.

"He's vanished!" he gasped in amazement. "Wow! So he was magic after all. But where's my wish?"

He raced back to the yard to see if it was waiting for him there...

...But as soon as Muck arrived all the other machines burst out laughing.

"Erm... what's that on your face, Muck?" giggled Dizzy.

"What... what? Is it mud?" he asked.

"No! You've got a cat face!" chuckled Scoop.

"Wow! I wonder if this has got anything to do with the magic dragon?" Muck said.

Dizzy, Scoop and Roley looked confused.

At Mrs Potts's house, Bob and Wendy were working in the loft. They'd found a lot of interesting things up there – clothes, toys and bits of material.

"Careful, Bob," said Wendy for the hundredth time. "You must stand on the wooden beams, or you'll..."

"Aaargh!" cried Bob, as his foot crashed through the floor.

"Oh dear!" exclaimed Mrs Potts. "Just look at my ceiling!"

"Can we fix it?" called Wendy.

"Er... yes, we can!" Bob replied in a quieter voice than usual.

Wendy called outside for Lofty's help.

"We might need some extra paint and plaster," she said. "Could you pop back to the yard to get them, just in case?"

"Erm, OK Wendy," said Lofty. But as Lofty returned to the yard, he saw the most scary sight – a dragon with big googly eyes!

"Roarrrr!" growled Spud the Dragon.

"Aaaarrrghhh!" cried Lofty.

A scared Lofty raced back to Mrs Potts's house as fast as he possibly could.

Bob had managed to free his leg and was repairing the plasterboard in Mrs Potts's ceiling, and Wendy was in the loft laying down rolls of insulating material.

"There you are, Mrs Potts," said Bob, at last. "We're all done, and we didn't need that extra paint and plaster after all."

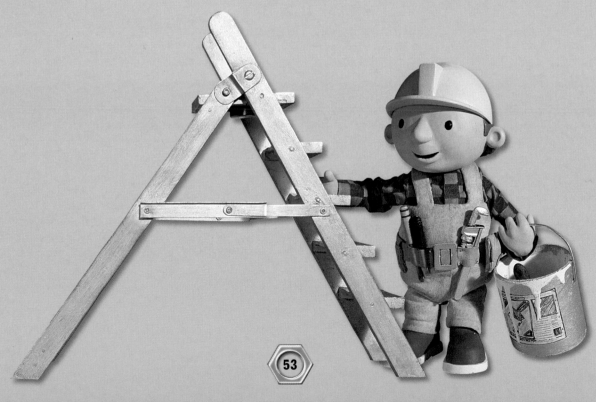

Just then, Lofty raced up.

"Oh, Wendy, oh, Bob!" he cried. "A... big... scary... dragon jumped out at me down the road!"

"Oh, Lofty!" said Wendy. "There aren't any dragons around here."

"There are... there is... I saw it," Lofty said. "It's got big googly eyes and everything!"

"It's all right," said Wendy. "Calm down. I'll tell you what, why don't Bob and I come with you and have a look?"

"Roarr!" said Spud, hopping down the road. "Ha ha hee hee... roarrrrr!"

"See... there it is!" said Lofty, who was ready to race in the opposite direction.

"That's no dragon," Wendy said. "I know that voice from somewhere."

"Uh, oh! I'm off!" said Spud, realizing he'd been found out. He jumped over the wall and ran into the woods.

"Come on, after him!" called Wendy.

Bob and Wendy chased the dragon through the woods, leaping over logs and darting between tree trunks.

As the dragon ran, the branches ripped off more and more of the costume, until...

"Woaaaahhh!" cried the dragon as he tripped, and his mask flew off.

"Ah ha! I thought so," said Wendy. "It's Spud!"

Wendy, Spud and Bob went back to the school-yard to tell Mrs Percival what had happened.

"My dragon costume!" she said. "There's no time to fix it before the school play tonight."

"Oww, I'm really sorry, Mrs Percival," said Spud, hanging his head.

"Wait – I've got an idea!" said Wendy, and she dashed out of the school-yard.

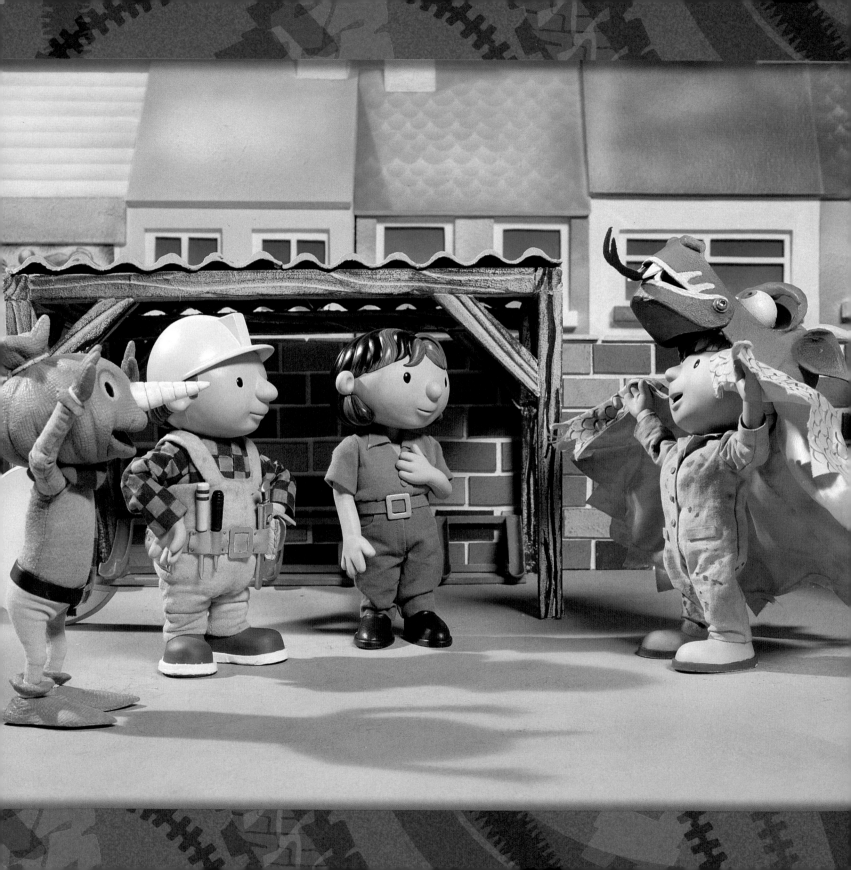

A while later...

"Hello, everyone!" roared a voice near the gate.

It was Wendy in the repaired dragon costume. She'd used some of the material in Mrs Potts's loft to mend the costume so it looked as good as new, and just as scary.

So scary, in fact, that Spud took one look at it and screamed.

"Argh! It's a real dragon!" he cried, as he raced out of the yard.

"Come back, Spud!" called Wendy.

"Hide, everyone, hide!" screamed Spud, running off down the road.

"Oh dear," said Wendy as she took off the mask. "It's only me, Spud!"

The End

Scruffty Works it Out

One morning, Bob was busy welding some pieces of metal together in his workshop.
"What's Bob making?" asked Muck.
"He's building a time capsule," Wendy replied.
"Everybody in the town is going to give Mr Ellis, at the museum, something to put into the capsule. Then we'll bury it outside the museum."
"Why?" asked Dizzy.
"So that people can dig up the capsule in a hundred years time and find out all about us," Wendy told her.

At the farm, Spud had a job to do. Farmer Pickles
had asked him to take a tray of eggs to the school.
"Oooh! They're very wobbly!" said Spud.
"Be careful not to break them, Spud!" said
Farmer Pickles.
Just then, Scruffty ran to Spud and jumped up.
"Ruff! Ruff!" he barked.
"Stop it!" cried Spud. "I'm working!"

Back at the yard, Bob had finished the time capsule.
He carried it out of the workshop for everyone to see.
  "We'll need Muck and Scoop to help us clear away
the rubble, Lofty to bury it and Dizzy to mix the cement
to stick the slab over the hole," Wendy explained to
the team.
  "Can we fix it?" shouted Scoop.
  "Yes, we can!" everyone replied.

Spud was walking slowly along the road, trying hard
not to break the eggs, when he met Squawk the crow.
  "Ark! Ark!" croaked Squawk.
Spud waved his arms to scare him away.
  "Shoo!" he shouted. But as he waved, the tray wobbled.
Splat! An egg smashed on the ground.
  "Ark! Ark!" laughed Squawk.
  "It's not funny!" said Spud, crossly.

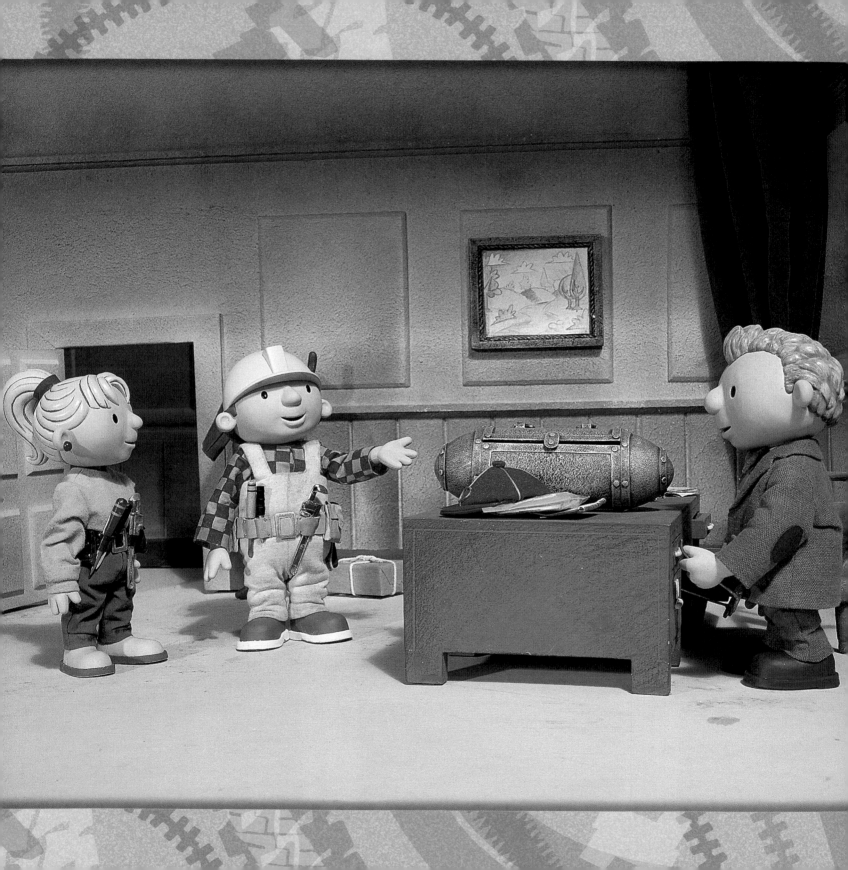

At the museum, Mr Ellis was thrilled with the time capsule.

"It's built to last forever!" Bob told him.

"I've already been given things to put in it," said Mr Ellis. "I've got today's newspaper, some stamps from the post office and a school cap from Mrs Percival."

Just then, Mr Bentley arrived with a model of the town hall, which he'd made out of matchsticks.

"Wow! That must have taken ages to build," said Bob.

"It took me twenty-eight and a half hours!" Mr Bentley told him proudly.

Outside the museum, Bob measured where the hole for the capsule should go. He put on his eye and ear protectors, and started to drill down into the paving stones.

"Dud, dud, dud, dud," went the drill.

Scoop and Muck got to work clearing the rubble away.

Just as Bob finished sweeping up, Farmer Pickles and Scruffty dashed towards them.

"Hold on! I've got something to go in the capsule," Farmer Pickles said as he handed over an old, green wellington boot!

"Thank you!" chuckled Bob. "In it goes."

Then Mr Dixon, the postman, turned up with a framed photograph of the town.

"That's great," said Bob, as he opened the capsule. "Goodness, it's filling up fast!"

Mr Dixon hurried off to finish his deliveries.
   Farmer Pickles tied Scruffty to the outside
of the museum, while he went inside to speak
to Mr Ellis.
   "Stay there!" he said.
   "Ruff! Ruff! Ruff!"
barked Scruffty.
   "Be a good boy now!"
said Farmer Pickles.

By the time Spud arrived at the school, most of the eggs were cracked and broken.

"It's not my fault, Mrs Percival," he said. "I've been chased by a dog and dive-bombed by a bird!"

"Poor old Spud!" chuckled Mrs Percival. "It's a good job we're having omelettes today!"

"Phew! That's all right then," said Spud as he skipped away.

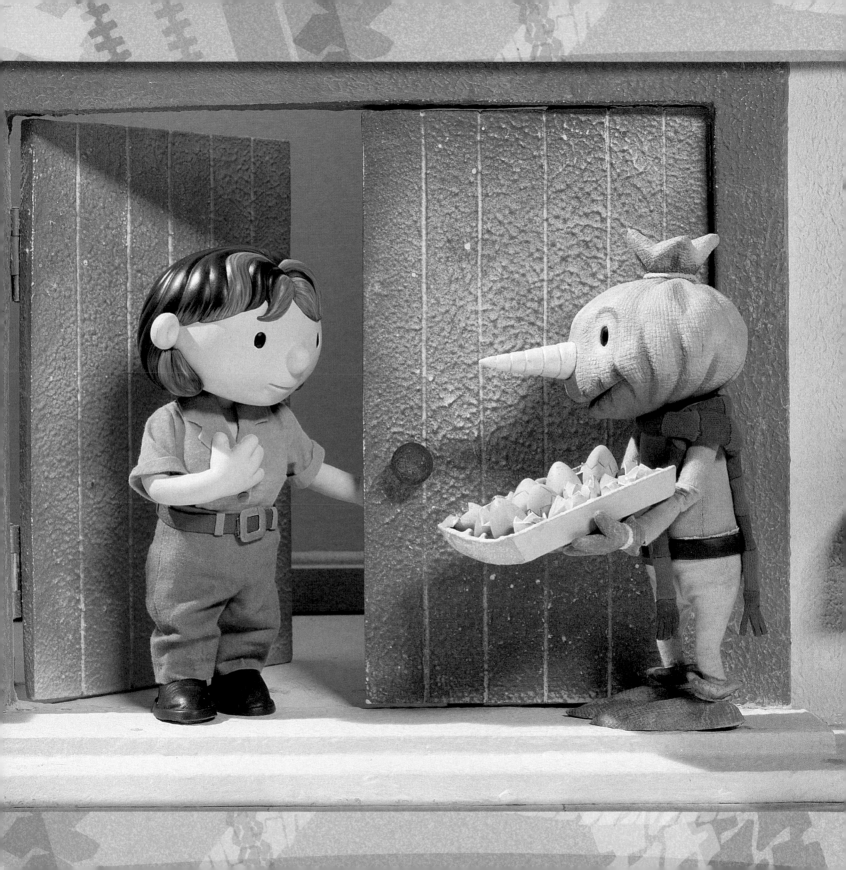

On his way home, Spud saw Scruffty tied up outside the museum.

"Ha, ha!" teased Spud. "You can't chase me now!"
Then he spotted the time capsule lying on the pavement.

"Wow! A treasure chest!" he cried.

"Ruff! Ruff!" barked Scruffty, frantically.

Spud picked up the capsule and staggered down the street.
He bumped into Travis further along the road.

"Oh, give us a lift!" he gasped.

"Hop in!" said Travis and trundled
off with Spud and the time
capsule in his trailer!

Spud opened the treasure chest and was very disappointed with what he found.

"This isn't real treasure!" he cried, as he tossed Farmer Pickles's wellington boot onto the road.

When Wendy and Bob came out of the museum, they found that the time capsule had gone.

"Oh, no! Where is it?" cried Bob.

"Ruff! Ruff!" barked Scruffty, as he tugged at his lead. Suddenly, it came undone and he ran off down the street. He came racing back with a boot.

"That's the wellington I put in the time capsule!" gasped Farmer Pickles.

"Ruff! Ruff!" barked Scruffty.

"I think he wants us to follow him," Farmer Pickles said, as he clipped the lead onto Scruffty's collar. Scruffty started sniffing, then bounded off down the road. Farmer Pickles had to run to keep up. Soon Scruffty stopped and Mr Ellis and Bob caught up.

"Oh, what a clever boy!" said Bob.

"He's found the book of stamps that was in the time capsule."

Scruffty set off again.

"Let's follow him!" shouted Bob.

Scruffty led Farmer Pickles into the countryside. He darted into a bush, dragging Farmer Pickles behind him.

"Look, you've found the school cap!" cried Farmer Pickles.

"I've had quite enough of being pulled about," he said, as he let Scruffty off the lead.

"Ruff! Ruff!" barked Scruffty and bounded off.

Further down the road, Spud was stuffing the time capsule with carrots, apples and corn on the cob!

"I'm going to dig a hole and bury my own food treasure chest right here!" he said.

Spud had dug his hole, and was about to bury his treasure chest, when Scruffty ran up and jumped on top of him.

"Ahh, get off me!" yelled Spud.

"Spud, what are you doing?" Farmer Pickles cried, when he, Bob and Mr Ellis caught up with Scruffty.

"It's my treasure chest and I'm burying it," Spud replied.

"That's not a treasure chest, Spud," said Bob. "It's Mr Ellis's time capsule!"

"Oh. Sorry, Bob" said Spud.

"You're very lucky Scruffty found you before you buried it!" said Bob.

They took the time capsule back into town, where a crowd
had gathered to watch Bob and the machines bury it.

Mr Bentley gave a speech, then Lofty carefully lowered the
capsule into the hole and Muck covered it with a large slab
of concrete.

"It won't be opened for a hundred years!" said Mr Ellis.

"Hurray!" cheered the crowd.

"There's someone very important that we haven't
mentioned, yet," Mr Ellis told the crowd.

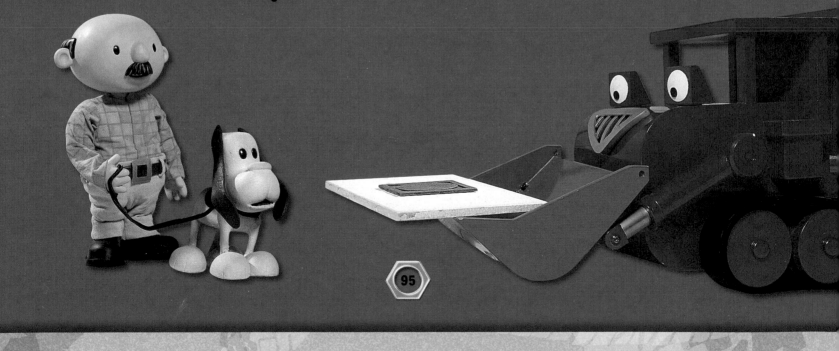

"This bone is a reward for clever Scruffty, who tracked down the missing time capsule," Mr Ellis said. "You're a hero!" "Ruff!" barked Scruffty as he chewed on his bone.

THE END!

Roley and the Rock Star

It was a very sunny morning. Bob looked at the barometer on his wall.

"Wow! It's going to be really hot today!" he said. Bob's fish, Finn, splashed the water with his tail. "I wish I could swim around all day and keep cool like you!" laughed Bob.

When Bob went out into the yard Wendy was loading tools into Muck's scoop.

"Morning, everyone!" said Bob.

"Morning, Bob!" Wendy and the machines replied.

"We've got two big jobs to do today," Bob told the machines. "I've got to build a pond in Mr Lazenby's front garden and Wendy's laying out a nature trail in the country park."

"Wow!" Roley rumbled. "Lennie Lazenby is the lead singer of the Lazers. They're my top band!"

"Come on then, team. Let's go!" said Bob.

101

When Wendy, Muck and Lofty arrived at the country park, Wendy studied her map.

"This is where the nature trail begins, so we'll need to put a signpost right here," she said, pointing at the ground.

Wendy dug a deep hole and Lofty carefully lowered the first signpost into the ground.

"What's a nature trail?" asked Muck.

"It's a path that people can follow to see all kinds of animals and plants," Wendy replied.

Further along the nature trail, Wendy and Muck were studying
the map, working out where the next signpost had to go.
When they weren't looking, a little duckling popped
out in front of Lofty.

"Quack!" it said.

"Ooooh!" Lofty wailed.

"What's the matter, Lofty?" called Wendy.

"A great big quacking thing just jumped out," he cried.

"A duck?" asked Wendy. But the duckling had
hopped back into the bushes.

"I can't see any ducks. You must be dreaming,
Lofty," said Muck.

Lofty kept a look-out for quacking things while Muck
and Wendy built a stile over a fence.
Suddenly two little ducklings waddled in front of Lofty
and Muck.
"Oooooh...er!" said Lofty as he ducked
behind a bush.

"Quack! Quack!"

went the ducklings.

Then another duckling appeared on the top of Lofty's jib!

"Lofty, you were right. Hello, little duckling!" said Wendy.

"Ooooh, Wendy! Take it away," he cried.

"You silly billy, Lofty," said Wendy. "The ducklings are more frightened of you than you are of them!"

"But I won't hurt them," said Lofty.

"I know, but sometimes people are scared of things for no reason at all. I wonder why they're so far away from the pond?" said Wendy. "Come on, team, let's take them back to the water."

Meanwhile, at Lennie Lazenby's house, Bob, Dizzy and Roley could hear loud music.

"Ooooh, it makes me want to dance!" cried Dizzy, as she got up and started to wiggle.

"Hey, Dizzy, let's rock and roll!" cried Roley.

"Toot! Toot!" chirped Bird, as he bobbed up and down on top of Roley's cab.

While Roley and Dizzy were dancing, Scoop dug
a big hole for the pond, and Bob lined it with
a waterproof sheet.

"I'll need lots of cement for the rockery around
the pond," Bob told Dizzy.

"Cement coming up!" giggled Dizzy.

Bob stuck the rocks around the edges of
the pond with Dizzy's cement.

"We'll wait for the cement to
set, then I'll add the finishing touch
– a fountain!" said Bob.

113

Lennie Lazenby came out into the garden just as Bob was
about to test the fountain.

"Hello, Mr Lazenby," said Bob.

"Hey, call me Lennie!" the rock star replied.

"Oh, er, right, Lennie," Bob replied.

"Oh, Lennie," said Roley, rushing up. "I really dig
your music!"

"Cool! Maybe we should have a jam some time," said Lennie.

"Wow! That would be great," said Roley.

Bob pressed the switch on the wall and
water bubbled up from the fountain.

114

"Groovy!" said Lennie. "Catch you later."

As Lennie walked away Roley sighed, "Isn't he cool?"

"Yes... but he doesn't look like the sort of person who would make jam," said Bob.

Roley burst out laughing. "Ha, ha, ha! Lennie doesn't make jam. Having a jam is when people get together to play music!"

"Oh, that kind of jam," said Bob, a bit embarrassed. "Silly me!"

Back at the country park, Wendy had found the duck pond.
"It's been so hot lately, the pond water has all dried up,"
she said.

"Poor little ducklings, they must have been looking for
a new home!" said Muck.

"Where's their mummy?" Lofty asked.

"I don't know, but I think we should look
after the ducklings until their mother
comes back," Wendy replied. "Let's see
if there's room for them at the pond that
Bob is building for Lennie Lazenby."

"Hi, Bob," said Wendy, when they arrived at Lennie
Lazenby's house.

"Hi, Wendy," said Bob.

"Quack! Quack!" went the little ducklings in Muck's scoop.

"They've lost their mother and their pond in the country park
has dried up," said Wendy. "Err,
Mr Lazenby do you think the ducklings
could stay in your pond?"

"Great idea! Ducks are, like, really
groovy!" said Lennie.

"Aw, thanks, Lennie!" said Muck as he tipped his shovel up and the ducklings slid into the pond.
Everyone gathered around to see if the ducklings liked their new home.

"Quack! Quack! Quack!"

went the ducklings as they splashed about in the water.
One little duckling hopped out of the pond and waddled up to Lofty.
"Ha, ha! You're not frightened of me any more," chuckled Lofty.

Just then, a big duck waddled across Lennie's lawn and hopped straight into the pond. The three ducklings gathered around her.

"That's the mother duck!" cried Dizzy.

"She must have been looking for a new home and now she's found one," said Bob.

"Hey, let's celebrate!" said Lennie. "Shall I sing my new single?"

"Yes, please! That would be brilliant!" squeaked Dizzy.

125

Lennie started to play his electric guitar. Bob, Wendy and all the machines danced around the garden to Lennie's music.

"Bob the Builder, can we fix it?" sang Bob.

"Bob the Builder, yes, we can!" Wendy sang back.

Soon all the machines had joined in the singing. Roley and Dizzy sang along especially loudly!

"Hey, groovy singing, Roley! Perhaps you could sing on my next album," said Lennie. "Wow! I'd love that," gasped Roley.

THE END!